THE RETURN OF
THE RITUAL

BY

DION FORTUNE

British Library Cataloguing-in-Publication Data
A catalogue record for this book is available from the
British Library

CONTENTS

DION FORTUNE

Dion Fortune was born Violet Mary Firth Evans in Bryn-y-Bia, Wales in 1890. She grew up in a household where Christian Science was devoutly practised (the pseudonym she later adopted was inspired by her family motto *Deo, non fortuna*, Latin for "by God, not fate'). At the age of twenty, Fortune suffered a nervous breakdown. After her recovery, she found herself drawn to the occult, joining the Theosophical Society and attending courses in psychology and psychoanalysis at the University of London. Here, she met Dr. Theodore Moriarty, who became her first esoteric teacher and inspired her first series of short stories, *The Secrets of Dr Taverner*.

From 1919 onwards, Fortune studied a range of occult and mystical topics, moving between various magical orders of the day and writing both fiction and non-fiction. Her most well-known book is *The Mystical Qabalah* (1935), an introduction to Hermetic Qabalah still regarded by occultists as one of the best books on magic ever written. *The Cosmic Doctrine* (1949), a summation of her basic teachings on mysticism, and *Psychic Self-Defense*, a manual on how to protect oneself from psychic attacks, also remain popular.

During World War II, Fortune led her own contribution

to the war effort on a magical level, with an extended meditation group aimed at aiding British pilots. She died from leukaemia in 1946 in Middlesex, London, aged 54. Her Society of the Inner Light continues to function to this day.

THE RETURN OF THE RITUAL

DION FORTUNE

It was Dr Taverner's custom, at certain times and seasons, to do what I should call hypnotise himself; he, however, called it 'going subconscious', and declared that, by means of concentration, he shifted the focus of his attention from the external world to the world of thought. Of the different states of consciousness to which he thus obtained access, and of the work that could be performed in each one, he would talk by the hour, and I soon learnt to recognise the phases he passed through during this extraordinary process.

Night after night I have watched beside the unconscious body of my colleague as it lay twitching on the sofa while thoughts that were not derived from his mind influenced the passive nerves. Many people can communicate with each other by means of thought, but I had never realised the extent to which this power was employed until I heard Taverner use his body as the receiving instrument of such messages.

One night while he was drinking some hot coffee I had given him (for he was always chilled to the bone after these performances) he said to me: 'Rhodes, there is a very curious affair afoot.'

I enquired what he meant.

'I am not quite sure,' he replied. 'There is something going on which I do not understand, and I want you to help me to investigate it.'

I promised my assistance, and asked the nature of the problem.

'I told you when you joined me,' he said, 'that I was a member of an occult brotherhood, but I did not tell you anything about it, because I am pledged not to do so, but for the purpose of our work together I am going to use my discretion and explain certain things to you.

'You know, I daresay, that we make use of ritual in our work. This is not the nonsense you may think it to be, for ritual has a profound effect on the mind. Anyone who is sufficiently sensitive can feel vibrations radiating whenever an occult ceremonial is being performed. For instance, I have only got to listen mentally for a moment to tell whether one of the Lhassa Lodges is working its terrific ritual.

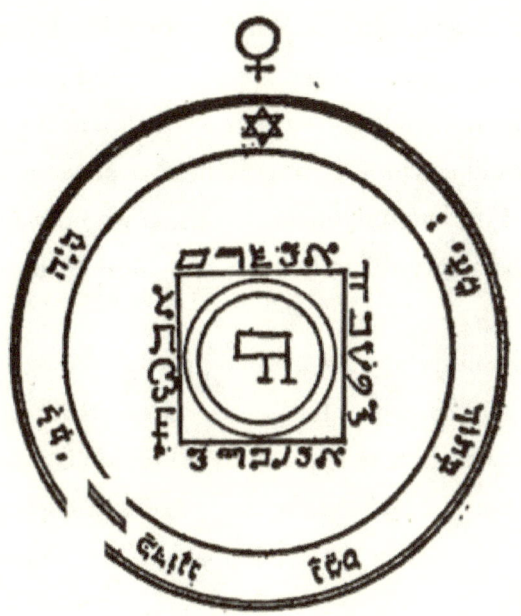

A RITUAL PENTACLE

'When I was subconscious just now I heard one of the rituals of my own Order being worked, but worked as no Lodge I have ever sat in would perform it. It was like a rendering of Tchaikovsky picked out on the piano with one finger by a child, and unless I am very much mistaken, some unauthorised person has got hold of that ritual and is experimenting with it.'

'Someone has broken his oath and given away your secrets,' I said.

'Evidently,' said Taverner. 'It has not often been done, but instances have occured, and if any of the Black Lodges, who would know how to make use of it, should get hold of the ritual the results might be serious, for there is great power in these old ceremonies, and while that power is safe in the hands of the carefully picked students whom we initiate, it would be a very different matter in those of unscrupulous men.'

'Shall you try to trace it?' I enquired.

'Yes,' said Taverner, 'but it is easier said than done. I have absolutely nothing to guide me. All I can do is to send round word among the Lodges to see whether a copy is missing from their archives; that will narrow our zone of search somewhat.'

Whether Taverner made use of the post or of his own peculiar methods of communication I do not know, but in a few days' time he had the information he required. None of the carefully guarded rituals was missing from any of the Lodges, but when search was made among the records at headquarters it was discovered that a ritual had been stolen from the Florentine Lodge during the middle ages by the custodian of the archives and sold (it was believed) to the Medici; at any rate, it was known to have been worked in Florence during the latter half of the fifteenth century. What became of it after the Medician manuscripts were dispersed at the plundering of Florence by the French was never known; it was lost sight of and was always believed to have been destroyed. Now, however, after the lapse of so many centuries someone was waking its amazing power.

As we were passing down Harley Street a few days later, Taverner asked me if I would mind turning aside with him into the Marylebone Lane, where he wished to call at a secondhand bookshop. I was surprised that a man of the type of my colleague should patronise such a place, for it appeared to be stocked chiefly with tattered paper-covered Ouidas and out-of-date piousness, and the alacrity with which the shopboy went to fetch the owner showed that my companion was a regular and esteemed customer.

The owner when he appeared was an even greater surprise than his shop; unbelievably dusty, his frockcoat, beard and face all appeared to be of a uniform grey-green, yet when he spoke his voice was that of a cultured man, and, though my companion addressed him as an equal, he answered as to a superior.

'Have you received any reply to the advertisement I asked you to insert for me?' asked Taverner of the snuff-coloured individual who confronted us.

'I have not; but I have got some information for you – you are not the only purchaser in the market for the manuscript.'

'My competitor being – ?'

'A man named Williams.'

'That does not tell us very much.'

'The postmark was Chelsea,' said the old bookseller with a significant look.

'Ah!' said my employer. 'If that manuscript should come into the market I will not limit you as to price.'

'I think we are likely to have a little excitement,' observed Taverner as we left the shop, its dust-covered occupant bowing behind us. 'The Chelsea Black Lodges have evidently heard what I heard and are also making a bid for the ritual.'

'You do not suppose that it is one of the Chelsea Lodges that has got it at the present moment?' I enquired.

'I do not,' said Taverner, 'for they would have made a better job of it. Whatever may be said against their morals, they are not fools, and know what they are about. No, some person or group of persons who dabbles in the occult without any real knowledge has got hold of that manuscript. They know enough to recognise a ritual when they see it, and are playing about with it to see what will happen. Probably no one would be more astonished than they if anything *did* happen.

'Were the ritual confined to such hands as those I should not be worried about it; but it may get into the possession of people who will know how to use it and abuse its powers, and then the consequences will be much more serious than you can realise. I will even go so far as to say that the course of civilisation would be affected if such a thing occurred.'

I saw that Taverner was profoundly moved. Regardless of traffic he plunged into the roadway, making a bee-line for his rooms.

'I would give any price for that manuscript if I could lay my hands on it, and if it were not for sale I would not hesitate to steal it; but how in the name of Heaven am I to trace the thing?'

We had regained the consulting-room, and Taverner was pacing up and down the floor with long strides. Presently he took up the telephone and rang up his Hindhead nursing home and told the matron that we should be spending the night in town. As there was no sleeping accommodation at the house in Harley Street, where he had his London headquarters, I guessed that a night of vigil was in contemplation.

I was fairly used to these watch-nights now; I knew that my duty would be to guard Taverner's vacated body while his soul ranged through outer darkness on some strange quest of its own and talked to its peers – men who were also able to leave their bodies at will and walk the starry ways with him, or others who had died centuries ago, but were still concerned with the welfare of their fellow men whom they had lived to serve.

We dined at a little restaurant in a back street off Soho,

where the head waiter argued metaphysics in Italian with Taverner between courses, and returned to our Harley Street quarters to wait until the great city about us should have gone to sleep and left the night quiet for the work we were about to embark upon. It was not till well after midnight that Taverner judged the time was suitable, and then he settled himself upon the broad consulting-room couch, with myself at his feet.

In a few minutes he was asleep, but as I watched him I saw his breathing alter, and sleep gave way to trance. A few muttered words, stray memories of his previous earthly lives, came from his lips; then a deep and sibilant breath marked a second change of level, and I saw that he was in the state of consciousness that occultists use when they communicate with each other by means of telepathy. It was exactly like 'listening in' with a wireless telephone; Lodge called to Lodge across the deeps of the night, and the passive brain picked up the vibrations and passed them on to the voice, and Taverner spoke.

The jangle of messages, however, was cut off in the middle of a sentence. This was not the level on which Taverner meant to work tonight. Another sibilant hiss announced that he had gone yet deeper into the hypnotic condition. There was a dead stillness in the room, and then a voice that was not Taverner's broke the silence.

'The level of the records,' it said, and I guessed what Taverner meant to do; no brain but his could have hit upon the extraordinary scheme of tracing the manuscript by examining the subconscious mind of the human race. Taverner, in common with his fellow psychologists, held that every thought and every act have their images stored in the person's subconscious mind, but he also held that records of them are stored in the mind of Nature; and it was these records that he was seeking to read.

Broken fragments of sentences, figures, and names, fell from the lips of the unconscious man, and then he got his focus and steadied to his work.

*'Il cinquecento, Firenze, Italia, Pierro della Costa,'*_ came a deep-level voice; then followed a long-drawn-out vibrating sound halfway between a telephone bell and the note of a 'cello, and the voice changed.

'Two forty-five, November the fourteenth, 1898, London, England.'

For a time there was silence, but almost immediately Taverner's voice cut across it.

'I want Pierro della Costa, who was reborn November the fourteenth, 1898, at two forty-five a.m.'

Silence. And then Taverner's voice again calling as if over a telephone: 'Hullo! Hullo! Hullo!' Apparently he received an answer, for his tone changed. 'Yes; it is the Senior of Seven

11

who is speaking.'

Then his voice took on an extraordinary majesty and command.

'Brother, where is the ritual that was entrusted to thy care?'

What answer was given I could not divine; but after a pause Taverner's voice came again. 'Brother, redeem thy crime and return the ritual whence it was taken.' Then he rolled over on to his side, and the trance condition passed into natural sleep, and so to an awakening.

Dazed and shivering, he recovered consciousness, and I gave him hot coffee from a thermos flask, such as we always kept handy for these midnight meals. I recounted to him what had passed, and he nodded his satisfaction between sips of the steaming liquid.

'I wonder how Pierro della Costa will effect his task,' he said. 'The present-day personality will probably not have the faintest idea as to what is required of it, and will be blindly urged forward by the subconscious.'

'How will it locate the manuscript?' I enquired. 'Why should he succeed where you failed?'

'I failed because I could not at any point establish contact with the manuscript. I was not on earth at the time it was stolen, and I could not trace it in the racial memories for the same reason. One must have a jumping-off place, you know.

Occult work is not performed by merely waving a wand.'

'How will the present-day Pierro go to work?' I enquired.

'The present-day Pierro won't do anything,' said Taverner, 'because he does not know how, but his subconscious mind is that of the trained occultist, and under the stimulus I have given it, will perform its work; it will probably go back to the time when the manuscript was handed over to the Medici, and then trace its subsequent history by means of the racial memories – the subconscious memory of Nature.'

'And how will he go to work to recover it?'

'As soon as the subconscious has located its quarry, it will send an impulse through into the conscious mind, bidding it take the body upon the quest, and a very puzzled modern young man may find himself in a difficult situation.'

'How will he know what to do with the manuscript when he has found it?'

'Once an Initiate, always an Initiate. In all moments of difficulty and danger the Initiate turns to his Master. Something in that boy's soul will reach out to make contact, and he will be brought back to his own Fraternity. Sooner or later he will come across one of the Brethren, who will know what to do with him.'

I was thankful enough to lie down on the sofa and get a couple of hours' sleep, until such time as the charwoman should disturb me; but Taverner, upon whom 'going subconscious' always seemed to have the effect of a tonic, announced his intention of seeing the sun rise from London Bridge, and left me to my own devices.

He returned in time to take me out to breakfast, and I discovered that he had given instructions for every morning paper and each successive edition of the evening ones to be sent in to us. All day long the stream of printed matter poured in, and had to be gone over, for Taverner was on the lookout for Pierro della Costa's effort to recover the ritual.

'His first attempt upon it is certain to be some blind lunatic outburst,' said Taverner, 'and it will probably land him in the hands of the police, whence it will be our duty as good Brethren, to rescue him; but it will have served its purpose, for he will, as it were, have "pointed" the manuscript after the fashion of a sporting dog.'

Next morning our vigilance was rewarded. An unusual case of attempted burglary was reported from St John's Wood. A young bank clerk of hitherto exemplary character had effected an entry into the house of a Mr Joseph Coates by the simple expedient of climbing on to the dining-room window-sill from the area steps, and, in full view of the entire street, kicking the glass out of the window. Mr Coates, aroused by the din, came down armed with a stick, which, however, was not required, the would-be burglar (who could give no explanation of his conduct) meekly waiting to be taken to the police station by the policeman whom the commotion he made had also attracted to the spot.

Taverner immediately telephoned to find out what time the case would be coming on at the police court, and we forthwith set out upon our quest. We sat in the enclosure reserved for the general public while various cases of wife-beaters and disorderly drunkards were disposed of, and I watched my neighbours.

Not far from us a girl of a different type from the rest of the sordid audience was seated; her pale oval face seemed to belong to another race from the irregular Cockney features about her. She looked like some mediaeval saint from an Italian fresco, and it only needed the stiff brocaded robes to complete the resemblance.

' "Look for the woman," ' said Taverner's voice in my ear. 'Now we know why Pierro della Costa fell to a bribe.'

The usual riff-raff having been dealt with, a prisoner of a different type was placed in the dock. A young fellow, refined, highly strung, looked round him in bewilderment at his unaccustomed surroundings, and then, catching sight of the olive-cheeked madonna in the gallery, took heart of grace.

He answered the magistrate's questions collectedly enough, giving his name as Peter Robson, and his profession as clerk. He listened attentively to the evidence of the policeman who had arrested him, and to Mr Joseph Coates, and when asked for his explanation, said he had none to give. In answer to questions, he declared that he had never been in that part of London before; he had no motive for going there, and he did not know why he had attempted to enter the window.

The magistrate, who at first had seemed disposed to deal leniently with the case, appeared to think that this persistent refusal of all explanation must conceal some motive, and proceeded to press the prisoner somewhat sharply. It looked as if matters were going hard with him, when Taverner, who had been scribbling on the back of a visiting card, beckoned an usher and sent the message up to the magistrate. I saw him read it, and turn the card over. Taverner's degrees and the Harley Street address were enough for him.

'I understand,' said he to the prisoner, 'that you have a friend here who can offer an explanation of the affair, and is prepared to go surety for you.'

The prisoner's face was a study; he looked round, seeking some familiar face, and when Taverner, well-dressed and of imposing appearance, entered the witness box, his perplexity was comical; and then, through all his bewilderment, a flash of light suddenly shot into the boy's eyes. Some gleam from the subconscious reached him, and he shut his mouth and awaited events.

My colleague, giving his name as John Richard Taverner,

doctor of medicine, philosophy and science, master of arts and bachelor at law, said that he was a distant relation of the prisoner who was subject to that peculiar malady known as double personality. He was satisfied that this condition was quite sufficient to account for the attempt at burglary, some freak of the boy's other self having led to the crime.

Yes, Taverner was quite prepared to go surety for the boy, and the magistrate, evidently relieved at the turn affairs had taken, forthwith bound the prisoner over to come up for judgment if called upon, and within ten minutes of Taverner's entry upon the scene we were standing on the steps of the court, where the Florentine madonna joined us.

'I don't know who you are, sir,' the boy was saying, 'nor why you should help me, but I am very grateful to you. May I introduce my fiancée, Miss Fenner? She would like to thank you, too.'

Taverner shook hands with the girl.

'I don't suppose you two have eaten much breakfast with this affair hanging over your heads,' he said. They admitted that they had not.

'Then,' said he, 'you must be my guests for an early lunch.'

We all packed into a taxi, and drove to the restaurant where the metaphysical head waiter held sway. Here Peter Robson immediately tackled Taverner.

'Look here, sir,' he said, 'I am exceedingly grateful to you for what you have done for me, but I should very much like to know why you did it.'

'Do you ever weave daydreams?' enquired Taverner irrelevantly. Robson stared at him in perplexity, but the girl at his side suddenly exclaimed:

'I know what you mean. Do you remember, Peter, the stories we used to make up when we were children? How we belonged to a secret society that had its headquarters in the woodshed, and had only to make a certain sign and people would know we were members and be afraid of us? I remember once, when we had been locked in the scullery because we were naughty, you said that if you made this sign, the policeman would come in and tell your father he had got to let us out, because we belonged to a powerful Brotherhood that did not allow its members to be locked in sculleries. That is exactly what has happened; it is your daydream come true. But what is the meaning of it all?'

'Ah, what, indeed?' said Taverner. Then turning to the boy: 'Do you dream much?' he asked.

'Not as a rule,' he replied, 'but I had a most curious dream the night before last, which I can only regard as prophetic in the light of subsequent events. I dreamt that someone was accusing me of a crime, and I woke up in a dreadful way about it.'

'Dreams are curious things,' said Taverner, 'both day dreams and night dreams. I don't know which are the stranger. Do you believe in the immortality of the soul, Mr. Robson?'

'Of course I do.'

'Then has it ever struck you the eternal life must stretch both ways?'

'You mean,' said Robson under his breath, 'that it wasn't all imagination. It might be – memory?'

'Other people have had the same dream,' said Taverner, 'myself among them.' Then he leant across the narrow table and stared into the lad's eyes.

'Supposing I told you that just such an organisation as you imagined exists; that if, as a boy even, you had gone out into the main street and made that sign, someone would have been almost certain to answer it?'

'Supposing I told you that the impulse which made you break that window was not a blind instinct, but an attempt to carry out an order from your Fraternity, would you believe me?'

'I think I should,' said the lad opposite him. 'At any rate, if it isn't true, I wish it were, for it appeals to me more than anything I have ever heard.'

'If you care to go deeper into the matter,' said Taverner, 'will you come this evening to my place in Harley Street, and then we can talk the matter over?'

Robson accepted with eagerness. What man would refuse to follow his daydreams when they began to materialise.

After we had parted from our new acquaintance, we took a taxi to St John's Wood and stopped at a house whose front ground-floor window was in process of being reglazed. Taverner sent in his card, and we were ushered into a room decorated with large bronze Buddhas, statuettes from Egyptian tombs, and pictures by Watts. In a few minutes Mr Coates appeared.

'Ah, Dr Taverner,' he said, 'I presume you have come about the extraordinary matter of your young relative who broke into my house last evening?'

'That is so, Mr Coates,' replied my companion. 'I have come to offer you my sincere apologies on behalf of the family.'

'Don't mention it,' said our host, 'the poor lad was suffering from mental trouble, I take it?'

'A passing mania,' said Taverner, brushing it away with a wave of his hand. He glanced round the room. 'I see by your books that you are interested in a hobby of my own, the ancient mystery religions. I think I may claim to be something of an Egyptologist.'

Coates rose to the bait at once.

'I came across a most extraordinary document the other

day,' said our new acquaintance. 'I should like to show it to you. I think you would be interested.'

He drew from his pocket a bunch of keys, and inserted one in the lock of a drawer in a bureau. To his astonishment the key pushed loosely through the hole, and he pulled the drawer open only to find that the lock had been forced off. He ran his hand to the back of the drawer, and withdrew it empty! Coates looked from Taverner to myself and back again in astonishment.

'That manuscript was there when I went to the police court this morning,' he said. 'What is the meaning of this extraordinary business? First of all a man breaks into my house and makes no attempt to steal anything, and then someone else breaks in and, neglecting many objects of value, takes a thing that can be of no interest to anyone but myself.'

'Then the manuscript which has been stolen is of no particular value?' said Taverner.

'I gave half-a-crown for it,' replied Coates.

'Then you should be thankful to have got off so lightly,' said Taverner.

'This is the devil, Rhodes,' he went on, as we re-entered the waiting taxi. 'Someone from a Chelsea Black Lodge, knowing Coates would be at the police court this morning, has taken that manuscript.'

'What is to be the next move?' I enquired.

'Get hold of Robson; we can only work through him.'

I asked him how he intended to deal with the situation that had arisen.

Cover of a notorious occult textbook of the turn of the century.

Madame Blavatsky, the most important female occultist of modern times.

Aleister Crowley in magical robes and with some of his ritual implements.

'Are you going to send Robson after the manuscript again?' I enquired.

'I shall have to,' said Taverner.

'I do not think there is the makings of a successful buccaneer in Robson.'

'Neither do I,' agreed Taverner; 'we shall have to fall back on Pierro della Costa.'

Robson met us at Harley Street, and Taverner took him out to dinner.

After dinner we returned to the consulting room, where Taverner handed round cigars, and set himself to be an agreeable host, a task in which he succeeded to perfection, for he was one of the most interesting talkers I have ever met.

Presently the talk led round to Italy during the Renaissance, and the great days of Florence and the Medici; and then he began to tell the story of one, Pierro della Costa, who had been a student of the occult arts in those days, and had brewed love philtres for the ladies of the Florentine court. He told the story with considerable vividness, and in great detail, and I was surprised to see that the attention of the lad was wandering, and that he was apparently pursuing a train of thought of his own, oblivious of his surroundings. Then I realised that he was sliding off into that trance condition with which my experience of my colleague had made me familiar.

Still Taverner talked on, telling the history of the old Florentine to the unconscious boy – how he rose to be custodian of the archives, was offered a bribe, and betrayed his trust in order that he might buy the favour of the woman he loved. Then, as he came to the end of the story, his voice changed, and he addressed the unconscious lad by name.

'Pierro della Costa,' he said, 'why did you do it?'

'Because I was tempted,' came the answer, but not in the voice in which the boy had talked to us; it was a man's voice, calm, deep, and dignified, vibrating with emotion.

'Do you regret it?' asked Taverner.

'I do,' returned the voice that was not the boy's voice. 'I have asked of the Great Ones that I may be permitted to restore that which I stole.'

'Thy request is granted,' said Taverner. 'Do that which thou has to do, and the blessing of the Great Ones be upon thee.'

Slowly the boy rolled over and sat up, but I saw at a glance that it was not the same individual who confronted us: a man, mature, of strong character and determined purpose, looked out of the boy's blue eyes.

'I go,' he said, 'to restore that which I took. Give me the means.'

We went round, he and Taverner and I, to the garage, and

25

got out the car. 'Which way do you want to go?' asked my colleague. The lad pointed to the south-west, and Taverner turned the car in the direction of the Marble Arch. Piloted by the man who was not Robson, we went south down Park Lane, and finally came out in the tangle of mean streets behind Victoria Station; thence we turned east. We pulled up behind the Tate Gallery, and the boy got out.

'From here,' he said, 'I go on alone,' and he disappeared down a side street.

Although we waited for a matter of half an hour, Taverner did not stop the engine. 'We may want to get out of here quick,' he said. Then, just as I was beginning to wonder if we were going to spend the night in the open, we heard running footsteps coming down the street, and Robson leapt into the car. That Taverner's precaution in not stopping the engine was justified was proved by the fact that close upon Robson's heels other footsteps sounded.

'Quick, Rhodes,' cried Taverner. 'Hang the rug over the back.' I did as I was bid, and succeeded in obscuring the number plate, and as the first of our pursuers rounded the corner, the big car leapt into its stride, and we drew clear.

No one spoke on the journey down to Hindhead.

We entered the sleeping house as quietly as might be, and as Taverner turned on the office lights, I saw that Robson carried a curious-looking volume bound in vellum. We did not tarry in the office, however, for Taverner led us through the sleeping house to a door which I knew led down to the cellar stairs.

'Come too, Rhodes,' said Taverner. 'You have seen the beginning of this matter, and you shall see the end, for you have shared in the risk, and although you.are not one of Us, I know that I can rely on your discretion.'

We passed down the spiral stone stairs and along a flagged passage. Taverner unlocked a door, and admitted us to a wine cellar. He crossed this, and unlocked a further door. A dim point of flame illumined the darkness ahead of us, swaying uneasily in the draught. Taverner turned on a light, and to my intense surprise I found myself in a chapel. High carved stalls were built into the walls on three sides, and on the fourth was an altar. The flickering light I had seen in the darkness came from the floating wick of a lamp hung above our heads as the centre point of a great Symbol.

Taverner lit the incense in a bronze thurible, and set it swinging. He handed Robson the black robe of an Inquisitor, and he himself assumed another one; then these two cowled figures faced one another across the floor of the empty chapel. Taverner began what was evidently a prayer. I could not gather its substance, for I am unable to follow spoken Latin. Then came a Litany of question and response, Robson, the London clerk, answering in the deep resonant voice of a man accustomed to intone across great buildings. Then he rose to his feet, and with the stately steps of a processional advanced to the altar, and laid thereon the ragged and mildewed manuscript he held in his hands. He knelt, and what absolution the sombre figure that stood over him pronounced, I cannot tell, but he rose to his feet like a man from whose shoulders a great burden has been rolled.

Then, for the first time, Taverner spoke in his native tongue. 'In all moments of difficulty and danger' – the booming of his deep voice filled the room with echoes – 'make this sign.' And I knew that the man who had betrayed his trust had made good and been received back into his old Fraternity.

We returned to the upper world, and the man who was not Robson bade us farewell. 'It is necessary that I should go,' he said.

'It is indeed,' said Taverner. 'You had better be out of England till this matter has blown over. Rhodes, will you undertake to drive him down to Southampton? I have other work to do.'

As we dropped down the long slope that leads to Liphook, I studied the man at my side. By some strange alchemy Taverner had woken the long dead soul of Pierro della Costa and imposed it upon the present-day personality of Peter Robson. Power radiated from him as light from a lamp; even the features seemed changed. Deep lines about the corners of the mouth lent a firmness to the hitherto indefinite chin, and the light blue eyes, now sunken in the head, had taken on the glitter of steel and were as steady as those of a swordsman.

It was just after six in the morning when we crossed the floating bridge into Southampton. The place was already astir, for a dock town never sleeps, and we enquired our way to the little-known inn where Taverner had directed us to go for breakfast. We discovered it to be an unpretentious public-house near the dock gates, and the potman was just drawing the bright curtains of turkey twill as we entered.

It was evident that strangers were not very welcome in the little tavern, and no one offered to take our order. As we stood there irresolute, heavy footsteps thundered down creaking wooden stairs, and a strongly built man wearing the four lines of gold braid denoting the rank of Captain entered the bar parlour. He glanced at us as he came in, and indeed we were sufficiently incongruous to be notable in such a place.

His eyes attracted my attention; he had the keen, outlooking gaze so characteristic of a seaman, but in addition to this he had a curious trick of looking at one without appearing to see one; the focus of the eyes met about a yard behind one's back. It was a thing I had often seen Taverner do when he wished to see the colours of an aura, that curious emanation which, for those who can see it, radiates from every living thing and is so clear an indication of the condition within.

Grey eyes looked into blue as the newcomer took in my companion, and then an almost imperceptible sign passed between them, and the sailor joined us.

'I believe you know my mother,' he remarked by way of introduction. Robson admitted the acquaintanceship, though I am prepared to swear he had never seen the man before, and we all three adjourned to an inner room for breakfast, which appeared in response to the bellowed orders of our new acquaintance.

Without any preamble he enquired our business, and Robson was equally ready to communicate it.

'I want to get out of the country as quietly as possible,' he said. Our new friend seemed to think that it was quite in the ordinary course of events that a man without luggage should be departing in this manner.

'I am sailing at nine this morning, going down the Gold Coast as far as Loango. We aren't exactly the Cunard, but if you care to come you will be welcome. You can't wear that rig, however; you would only draw a crowd, which I take it is what you don't want to do.'

He put his head through a half-door which separated the parlour from the back premises, and in response to his vociferations a little fat man with white chin whiskers appeared. A consultation took place between the two, the newcomer being equally ready to lend his assistance. Very shortly a suit of cheap serge reach-me-downs and a peaked cap were forthcoming, these being, the sailor assured us, the correct costume for a steward, in which capacity it was designed that Peter Robson should go to sea.

Leaving the inn that the mysterious Fellowship had made so hospitable to us, we took our way to the docks, and passing through the wilderness of railway lines, cranes, and yawning gulfs that constitute their scenery, we arrived at our companion's ship, a rusty-sided tramp, her upper works painted a dirty white.

We accompanied her captain to his cabin, a striking contrast to the raffle outside: a solid desk bearing a student's shaded lamp, a copy of Albrecht Dürer's study of the *Praying Hands*, a considerable shelf of books, and, perceptible beneath the all-pervading odour of strong tobacco, the faint spicy smell that clings to a place where incense is regularly burnt. I studied the titles of the books, for they tell one more of a man than anything else; *Isis Unveiled* stood cheek by jowl with *Creative Evolution* and two fat tomes of Eliphas Levi's *History of Magic*.

On the drive back to Hindhead I thought much of the strange side of life with which I had come in contact.

Yet another example was afforded me of the widespread

ramifications of the Society. At Taverner's request I looked up the sea captain on his return from the voyage and asked him for news of Robson. This he was unable to give me, however; he had put the lad ashore at some mudhole on the West Coast. Standing on the quay stewing in the sunshine he had made the Sign. A half-caste Portuguese had touched him on the shoulder, and the two had vanished in the crowd. I expressed some anxiety as to the fate of an inexperienced lad in a strange land.

'You needn't worry,' said the sailor. 'That sign would take him right across Africa and back again.'

When I was talking the matter over with Taverner, I said to him: 'What made you and the captain claim relationship with Robson? It seemed to me a perfectly gratuitous lie.'

'It was no lie, but the truth,' said Taverner. 'Who is my Mother, and who are my Brethren but the Lodge and the Initiates thereof?'

*The fifteenth century, Florence, Italy, Peter della Costa.